# MOLE

## and the newspaper

For Flo, Tommy,

Lucas and Hugo

M.D.

MYRIAD BOOKS LIMITED
35 Bishopsthorpe Road, London SE26 4PA

First published in 2001 by
MIJADE PUBLICATIONS
16-18, rue de l'Ouvrage
5000 Namur-Belgium

© Laurence Bourguignon, 2001
© Michaël Derullieux, 2001

Translation: Lisa Pritchard

ISBN  1 84746 032 1

Printed in China

# MOLE
## and the newspaper

Laurence Bourguignon
& Michaël Derullieux

Translation: Lisa Pritchard

MYRIAD BOOKS LIMITED

Mole was strolling in the garden. Somebody had
left a newspaper near the deckchair.

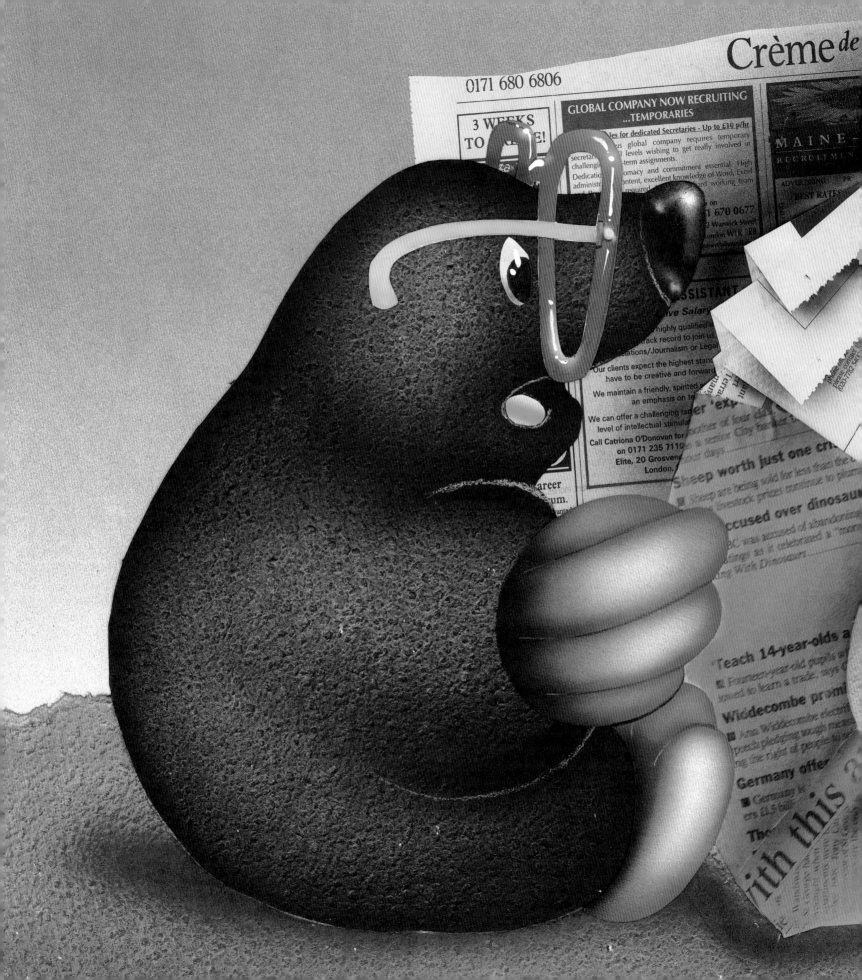

"I'll sit down and read it," said Mole.
He read it very quickly.
"It's going to be sunny, and rainy, and windy."

Just then a big raindrop fell, and another, and another.
"I told you so," said Mole.

"I don't like getting wet.
It's a good thing I found
this newspaper."

Bernard: brought in by
edwood to help out bid

Sometimes Mole was bored when it rained.
But not today.

He started to fold the paper. How many birds
did he make?

It rained and rained. The water was rising.
Mole didn't want to get wet.

Mole had a brilliant idea. "I'm off!
I'm going to find a country where
the sun always shines."

When Mole got there, he was
very happy. "That's better,"
he laughed.

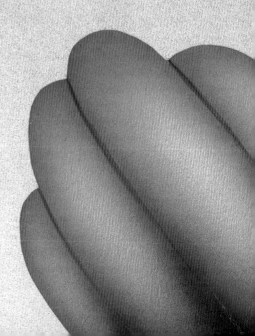

"And look, it's windy too.
I told you so, didn't I?"